In the Embrace of Darkness

GROUND ZERO

IN THE EMBRACE OF DARKNESS

By
Cory Alexander K. Rolle

Contents

Preface

Ground Zero is based on a child who lost his parents and his sanity. Having lost everything, the character, David, wonders in life with the devil on his shoulders and a death list. Lost in society, David encounters the key characters that will enlighten him and reveal the truth that he has been searching for. Young and deceived, with a broken heart and a corrupted mindset, he is unable to receive help or give love. He walks a path that many refuse to travel, in search of answers and healing. David will face adversity alone with a heart on a path to destruction and engulfed by darkness. All alone in the cold-hearted world without the support of others. David will encounter numerous obstacles and meet strange characters that will change his life!

CHAPTER 1

LOST CHILD

I lived in a peaceful country and had a family everyone wanted. We laughed together, worked together, and fought through the toughest times together. It was like I was in a perfect dream. I started following in my family's footsteps; I was active, responsible, and outspoken. However, reality soon became a nightmare.

One night, I overheard an argument between my mother and father. I decided to investigate the situation, but suddenly, I heard a thud and a gunshot. As I creeped out to see what had happened, I saw my mother and father lying on the floor in a puddle of blood. Someone had shot my parents, but I didn't know who would do such a thing. From that moment, I was traumatized. My only two parents were gone, and I had no one to turn to. I swore to kill that person who murdered my parents. As I sat beside my parents, tears stung my eyes and suddenly came out, but I was consumed by hatred.

Later that morning, my uncle Jimmy and cousins came by to visit. They came in and noticed a puddle of blood by the door step, so they rushed in to see what happened. When they came in, I was sitting beside my parents as if they were still alive. My heart was filled with hatred and pain. The only thing on my mind was revenge. However, I couldn't let my family know what I was planning. I only showed my sorrow, but not the vengeance that increasingly burned like a fire deep inside my heart.

The ambulance came to pick up the bodies of my parents, but they were nothing but corpses. All I could remember was my father's warm hug and my mother's beautiful smile. I could still feel my father's hugs and visualize my mother's smile, but sadly, they were just memories. Just thinking about it increased the fire in my heart. With clenched fists, I unleashed my fury on the pile of sheet rock stacked together in the closet. I rapidly punched through two at once and continued. Every punch seemed to release the anger isolated inside my heart, but it actually made it worse. Eventually, I got through all of the sheet rocks and left a massive hole in them. Blood dripped from my hands like I had killed someone, and it felt like a car rolled over my hands. Moving them felt impossible, but I made it possible. I needed my hands to kill the person who murdered my beloved parents.

Darkness corrupted my heart, my soul, and my mind. My hatred was deeper than the ocean, and the tears that I hid filled the rivers. All those sweet dreams and peaceful nights turned into restless nights of thinking, isolating my emotions and sitting in the dark. All the love, happiness, and sweet thoughts were gone and replaced with pain, nothing but pain! I was at ground zero with the devil by my side. My life was slowly fading away—chains breaking, love fading, and a young boy craving the death of others. I started to question God, "Why did this have to happen to me? Why me, and why now?" I hated my life, and I wanted to leave this world.

As I opened my eyes to a new day, my Uncle Jimmy and cousins left without saying goodbye. I was all alone with no one to rely on or talk to. I walked into the room where my parents were murdered. Blood stains splattered the walls. A Bullet casing and a pair of gloves were on the floor. I saw my parent's wedding rings tied together.

What a sweet thing, I thought, so I picked up the rings and held them close no matter what.

Suddenly, I felt a warm, scaly hand on my back. I could feel the presence of something diabolical. I turned around and saw the devil. My motor system shut down, and my heart rate decreased. This was not the first time we had an encounter. However, that first encounter was in my dream. As I stood there, the devil told me all my wishes could come true only if I gave him my soul. He could find, torture, and kill my parent's killer. Furthermore, he could even revive my parents if I took the life of another. However, by taking that person's life, a chain reaction will occur. Everything would return to normal if I completed the task and sold my soul. I accepted his offer without hesitation. My soul was now his, and it was time to hunt.

SLIPPING AWAY

Lost my bearings a moment here
Driven by pain and hatred rather than fear
No one knew how I felt or really reacted
The horrifying sights still under closed eyelids
The memory still attached in mind

And back then only one solution
I wanted to find
Felt like a dream, an illusion, a thick mist
I punched through it all, but it left me with
bloody knuckles and hurt wrists
Why was it added to my story?
Why did it have to be me?
In a split second I was thrown
to the edge of destruction

A ticking time bomb of corruption
But I controlled my emotions,
not letting temptation capture me
Now, with new eyes I see
Never said my mind changed;
it's hard to forget
The memory is needed to fuel my success
further, so I don't regret it
Just wish it wasn't like this some days
Set it all different,
and see the change in various ways
But it's all part of my life
I must now work with passion and
determination, not sinister intent or strife

Don't ever change, be you
Be a well-rounded individual not forever
pessimistic and blue
There's so much that can come
out of one person
Despite people's negativity, feedback or cursing
It is up to you who you decide to be
Best part is... it's free.

Seven days, seven nights, one person, and a bunch of death wishes. As time flew by, I started to wonder if my parents actually loved me. I wasn't showered by their love. I got a roof over my head and a meal per day, but I knew it wasn't enough. I starved numerous times, but I was happy to be alive. However, I felt alienated. Mother spent most of her free time with her associates and cheating on dad. Father was another mess; he spent most of his time getting drunk and having fun with his friends. He always made excuses when I wanted to spend time with him. "Maybe next time, boy," was always his response. I gave up and accepted it. I felt horrible, but I remained optimistic for the best. I never got the chance to say goodbye, nor I love you. Sadly, time isn't on anyone's side, so I'll have to endure and live with it. Everything seemed to be picture-perfect to everyone, but sadly, behind closed doors, everything was a disaster.

One day, I overheard someone talking about severing a bond in the house, but I wasn't able to hear clearly. They said they wanted it to be like nothing ever happened. At that moment, my body froze, and I was unable to move. Seconds later, a tranquilizing dart struck me, and I can't remember what happened that day until now. Was I the target? Why were my parents killed? Am I supposed to be the one in the body bag? It's so confusing; life is hectic, and I'm all alone. What happened to all of my friends and loved ones? Where did everyone go, and why had I lost everything in the blink of an eye? I despise this cruel world!

The following day, I gathered a few weapons and ammunition to start the blood fest. The devil told me I had two choices: Either I killed my uncle or the guy who killed my parents. Without hesitation, I chose the person who killed my parents. However, I had to find that person first. I faced a new chapter in my life, uncertain of its outcome. I felt torn apart. The mirror showed a stranger, a monster. But I believed in fate: one mission, one target, one chance. Everything changed in a flash, and I lost control. The devil was my only friend, and we defied the world. The child everyone once knew vanished. My name is David, and I will cleanse the earth!

Sunny days, dark nights, and a world engulfed with negativity. Is it wrong to personally remove all the sinners from the world? I wished to purge until my heart stopped bleeding. I could sense the "old me" struggling to resurface, but it was too late for him. I was a new version of myself, a vessel of pain. Pain that feels good to release. Am I lost, or is this who I truly am? I wondered. When will my parents hold me again? It felt like I was missing something! My strength increased by the hour. Each day, my memories deteriorate, and the void in my heart increases. I wished someone could end my life before I brought an innocent citizen to his or her early demise. I believed I was not fit to be in this world, but before I left, I had to cleanse this world!

I wondered if my parents were watching me from above or below. Who knows, and who cares? Would the light shine upon me once more? I wondered how it felt to be normal. As the days went by, I tended to have a sharp pain where my heart was located. It was like someone lodged an object between two gears that were trying to turn. When I lay in bed, staring at the ceiling, I felt a weird presence reaching out to me. But I was skeptical, so I ignored it. Every night, it was the same.

A new day had come, and I had to stop wasting time and start hunting. I was curious why I suddenly got this opportunity, but it no longer mattered. I decided to explore the town and look for clues. I didn't know where to begin, but I couldn't stay inside, dwelling and weeping. Shortly after, I saw an old man who lived a few houses down from where I live, so I decided to ask him a few questions. As I approached him, he opened his eyes and looked at me with compassion as if he knew what happened. Before I got to say a word, he told me, "Walk away from the path you are on before you lose yourself. Do not destroy yourself because of what happened. I can sense something diabolical in your heart. Release it before it's too late, David! Your parents were good individuals, but you must not figure out the truth behind it all. Save yourself and start a new life. Death is near, and what you'll uncover will shatter what is left of your heart. Explore the world, discover new things, meet new people, leave everything behind, and learn how to love again. I'm sorry, but this will be the last time we speak again. I'm afraid I have said too much, and now I'm a target. Be safe, David. Maybe one day we'll catch up, bulla."

As the old man lectured me, I began to cry. I could not see due to the amount of tears I shed. I used my shirt to wipe my face, but suddenly, the old man vanished. I've never had an encounter like that before. It felt like I released a hidden card on the deck that would change everything.

Tears, blood, and sweat shed as my subconscious mindset evaluated everything that occurred and what I could encounter. The devil told me to head west toward the hidden beach where my parents met each other. "There will be a note that will uncover a bit of history. Go now!" said the devil. I was confused. Why am I the only one lost in society? I'm lost, and I don't know how to find my way back into reality. I had no source of transportation, so I began walking. As I walked towards my destination, I began to reminisce about my mother's smile and the perfume she wore. I felt a presence like before, but it was different. I felt a touch on my shoulder, and I was pulled back! I instantly turned around, but I didn't see anyone. Why was I reminiscing about my mother at a time like this, and why was I constantly feeling those weird presences? Was I going insane, or was I that mentally unstable? Finally, I reached my destination. It took me roughly thirty minutes to get to the beach. I made my way toward the beach, and I felt that strange presence I had encountered when I was in my room staring at the ceiling. Perhaps this was a sign or something to frighten me. I was unsure, but I had to figure out why the devil wanted me to investigate. As I walked on the sand, the atmosphere got dense, and my chest got heavy. It was as if I triggered an event that could possibly change the path I was on. I continued advancing, and as I got further on the beach, I saw a large palm tree. Something seemed odd about it, so I stared at it for a bit. Suddenly, I was pinned to the ground, and my arms were barred in the sand. A child appeared and told me, "Walk away, brother. I know you are lost, but do not continue traveling on this treacherous path you are on! Abandon this path because you are damaging yourself even more. The 'old you' is scared and is surrounded by darkness! Please stop while you can before it is too late. Despite the fact that you don't know who I am, I love you, David."

CHAPTER 2

A BROKEN HEART

My heart broke into pieces and shattered upon impact. I attempted to remove the void that engulfed my heart, but I didn't know how to make it possible. I wanted to fix what I had done, but I craved revenge and to hear my parent's killer scream. Is it wrong to seek revenge and to allow the devil to control my steps in life? I'd lost my mind and my loved ones. My heart was on ground zero. My heart was like a dying ember that I tried to protect from the harsh winds of life. But I knew it was futile to resist the inevitable, especially when I was walking on a path of destruction. Why did I struggle to heal my heart when I had lost the most precious part of it? It felt like someone stole my soul but left me alive in this cruel world. When I was depressed, I heard a voice in my heart that encouraged me. "No matter how crucial the situation is, remember to remain calm. Face adversity and release the lion hidden inside of you. You are limitless, and I will always be with you inside this dark prison. I may not be able to assist you on your journey; however, know that I love you, and I am proud of you no matter what happens! Shine bright, and remember, you are unique. The answer you are searching for is right in front of you. Have faith and follow the clues!"

How could I ask God for forgiveness when I did not know how to forgive myself or others? How could I ask to be enlightened and be brought into the light if my heart is engulfed in darkness and the devil is on my shoulders? Why ask for help if I didn't know how to receive help? My heart was slowly meeting its demise. Should I give up or continue riding the wave? A death list and eyes filled with rage. Could I be contained? Would someone stop me from my rampage, and when will it end? Being truly content is a myth. To have an individual that truly loves you and supports you is rare. Love is a four-letter word that persuades people to attempt unthinkable things for others, but we live in a world corrupted by money and materialistic things. Sometimes, I wonder why I try to love others when I'm left alone in the end. I wished to end it all, one bullet and a gun, an empty vessel and a restless soul. One day, I would be "happy" and "free."

The tension that held me down was gone, and I could move again, but I stayed face down on the sand, thinking about life. Why did I feel a connection to that little boy? None of this made any sense! Why did I have to suffer so much? I never asked to be born into this cold world or to endure this pain! Was this a trial or punishment from our beloved heavenly father, and what horrible crime I committed? I could feel the pressure in my veins increasing as each minute went by. Life is filled with mysterious things; people tend to change, and you can lose everything you own and love within seconds. However, I had a goal: to redeem my parents no matter what! I would not rest until I cleansed my soul and watched my parent's killer suffer until he or she met their demise. From then on, I was not David. I was Abaddon. All I knew was destruction and hatred, and I had to follow the path I had chosen. This world would burn, and blood would stain the ground. I could not turn back then, and time was running out, so it was all or nothing.

What are demons doing in the land of the living? Are they here to wreak havoc on people's lives or to grant us our wishes in exchange for our souls? We live only to die, and we die only to live. What a way to exist! Hope is for the foolish, yet hope is what drives people to go further. Was I truly lost in society? Was I toxic and full of hatred? Was I wrong for expressing how I feel? No matter what I do now, I'll be judged regardless. I shed tears, sweat, and blood without hesitation, but my body was numb, and my heart was shrouded in darkness. Why do I cry if my heart is corrupted? I don't understand anything anymore. What a cruel world we live in, and I'm part of it.

I finally got up and decided to get closer to the palm tree. As I got closer, I noticed a note with two names and a heart between them. Those two names were my parent's name, "Mary plus Kapril forever." Tears instantly flowed out, similar to a waterfall. All the memories of me and my parents bombarded me without hesitation. The days my parents spent arguing and when we sat on the beach and gazed at the stars until midnight are just memories now. It's strange how I desire to purge but desire love and compassion. Was something truly wrong with me, or was it a sign from God to revert back to the old me?

I remembered my father's conflicts with the mafia, my mother's affairs with her colleagues, and a few vague details about someone named Jacob. Everything was being revealed so fast, but it was hard to grasp everything at once. Why was the name "Jacob" so important, and why did I remember it so suddenly? Was he the other half of myself that I was missing or someone who could change the course of my life? Until I could solve this mystery, I had to keep walking on my journey. All this information was revealed, but I still didn't know what to do or where to go from here. All I got were broken hints that gave me more questions than answers. My mind was cluttered, and I was unsure of my goals, so I decided to walk back home. Time had passed, and I made no progress.

A broken heart, a soulless body, and two kingdoms without the two keys. When will the corruption end? I was living a life full of lies, and all I knew was destruction. How could someone look at me as a human being? Why would someone accept me for who I am if I don't accept myself or love myself? I don't think the world is corrupted; I think I'm the one that's messed up, and also the people surrounding me. There are so many fine errors in life, and I'm one of those errors, such as life. My life was crumbling day by day, and I was adding fuel to the fire without noticing it. Life is filled with numerous mysteries that I'm unable to understand due to my intellect. Every hour, a life is created, but every five minutes, a life is taken away without hesitation.

As I walked home alone in the dark, the devil minion appeared and told me, "The clock is ticking, and blood needs to be shed!" I understood what my task was, but I lost my edge. It was like I had no choice anymore, or I never had a choice to walk on my own terms from birth. Was it my destiny to become a cold-hearted killer and rain destruction upon the world? Sadly, I had no choice but to go back to the person I once was. As I got closer to my house, I remembered an old man who advised me to change my course. His kind words left me speechless and gave me more questions. What caught me off guard was the fact that he said, "Death is near, and what you'll uncover will shatter what is left of your heart." Such a blunt way to warn me, but how did that old man know so much in such a short time? Would I ever find out why he knew so much about me, or would I remain in confusion forever?

The old man lived by himself, so I got curious and decided to enter his home. As I approached his doorstep,

I noticed the door knob was broken off. Suddenly, I felt a dark aura as I entered the building, and the scent of death consumed the house. The scent reminded me of the horrible night my parents were murdered. Shortly after I walked down the hallway, I noticed the old man sitting down on the chair in the living room. I wanted to analyze him properly, but as I turned my head, my body froze, and a young male stood in front of me. This experience is similar to when I was on the beach and was unable to move my body. The young boy looked exactly like me but with brown eyes. The young boy told me, "David, you need to alter your course before you reach a point of no return. It's not too late to run away from this disaster and stop placing a heavy burden on your chest because you're already a ticking time bomb. You are incomplete because of the deal you made with the devil, and I am your brother. You never met me, but Mom and Dad told me a lot about you. We're together in limbo, and everything is ok! Please run away, brother. I won't be able to save you. Oh, he's coming for me. I'm sorry, brother, but we may never meet like this again until you remove the demon off your shoulder. Goodbye, brother. I love you, and be happy!".

The scent of death bombarded the house, my body started trembling, and I got closer to the old man who gave me valuable advice. He told me, "I'm afraid I said too much, and now I'm a target. Be safe, David. Maybe one day we'll catch up bulla." Those were the last words the old man said to me before he died. Was I the reason this man died? He was such a generous man, and by placing his life on the line, he enlightened me and gave me a fighting chance.

I felt like a complete mess. Why did everything around me tend to die so suddenly? I constantly blamed myself for the events that occurred around me. It didn't matter what I did; I'd always be a black sheep in this life. I've been through so many trials and tribulations that sometimes, I wish to be in the sky to know how it feels to fly and be free. I'm not afraid to die or say goodbye to someone, but I'm scared to say hello. If poison were a person, it would be me! Each encounter will deteriorate a person's flesh slowly and eat away the core until there's nothing left. I felt like nothing but a toxicant that brought harm to innocent individuals. Why was I being so emotional about a situation that was altering my goal? Was that what it felt like to have compassion toward an individual or an object? It's been so long since I've felt loved or truly cared for something.

So much time had passed, and I hadn't committed a murder as yet. Would this be a breach in the deal I made, or was it not the right time to purge? Whatever it was, I hoped I could fulfill my duty and end this nightmare. The diabolical servants were observing my movements, and if I failed to comply with the agreement I made with the devil, I would lose it all. However, hadn't I lost it all already? Why don't I give up now and allow the events to occur on it's own? My heart, mind, body, and soul were not in sync. My mind was fixated on completing the task that I'd been given. My heart desired love and compassion, to understand what I lost and gained, and to connect to the people I love. My body acted on its own accord because my heart and mind did not sync. This is the reason I was unable to move freely sometimes or complete certain tasks. My soul desired to connect with my heart, mind, and body; however, during that period of my life, my soul was unable to sync due to the errors I made. Until I placed all of the pieces together and solved this mystery, my soul would be adrift in a void.

It seemed that whatever action I took, every movement would be recorded, and if I altered my course, someone I loved would die, or something negative would occur. I was neither unable to counteract the devil's plans nor gain support from others due to the barrier I created to isolate myself. The world will be bombarded by lightning bolts, blood will be splattered on the streets, and the scent of death will destroy the ozone layer. To outsmart a demon, I must become one, fight fire with fire! These unpredicted events have placed a major strain on my body, mind, and soul. I just wanted to be happy and to be loved. However, life is full of mysteries, and everything happens for a reason. Sometimes, you desire something and ask for it, but when you receive it, you may realize the thing you asked for isn't something you need. Every action comes with a consequence, which could be positive or negative. You are the only one responsible for your actions, and if you choose to run away rather than overcome the situation, life will bombard you.

I had to abandon my emotions so I could fulfill my objectives. Killing someone while being emotional would compromise and counteract my actions, which would jeopardize the mission. Did I really have what it takes to complete the mission and end this nightmare? As I advanced further on the path of destruction, my soul became harder to grasp!

CHAPTER 3

MEMORIES

After contemplating my path in life and reminiscing about those inspirational words the old man gave me, I decided to leave the house instead of procrastinating. I had wasted too much time wandering around, picking up any given detail that may lead me astray. As I walked through the hallway, a bright light flashed around me, and seconds later, I was unsure of my whereabouts. Everything was so bright, and there was not a soul in sight. I wondered if I had finally lost my mind. Was I all alone, and why was I here? A faint figure stood in front of me, shrouded in darkness. I could not make out any features, no lips, no sound. Had I lost my mind? Tears streamed down my face as I stared at the figure. I knew I was on a path of destruction, chosen to commit horrible things to avenge my parents' death, but I was terrified. I was just a young boy. Why couldn't I complete this simple mission and be happy again? I felt worthless, unable to do anything right. Tears continued to drop off my face as I stood near the figure.

Suddenly, I felt a warm touch, but there was no one near me. The figure remained still, so I could not understand what was happening.

"David, stop crying. Everything will be okay, my son," a voice spoke to me, but I did not recognize it. Yet, I felt a sense of calm and comfort, as if an angel had lifted the burden from my shoulders and given me hope.

Why was this happening all of a sudden? Was this another vision or test? Then, I saw him—my father. I froze in shock. I had held him and my mother as they bled to death. How could he be alive? This was too much to bear! My father held on to me and told me, "My time with you is limited, my son. I've brought you to this void to protect you from those who haunt you. I'm unable to assist you with your journey in the land of the living due to my death, and the devil is restricting my movements. I've watched you from above, and I notice you're falling into a pit of darkness. Do not feel responsible for me and your mother's death. It's our fault we allowed you to witness such a traumatizing event. We got caught up with the wrong company and foolishly trusted someone close to us. Just know not to trust a family member with a tattoo on his chest".

All of this information bombarded my mind as I tried to comprehend all of this. "Father, I guess I'm wrong for choosing this path, and did I disappoint you and Mother? Why haven't you told me about my brother, Jacob? Who is that old man that lived a few houses from us? The old man told me he knew who I was without hesitation. I never saw that man in my life. What are you hiding from me?" I asked my father the questions that I had been pondering on.

My father shrugged his head and told me that I was walking in circles. "David, I loved your mother unconditionally, and I will admit we weren't the best couple. We fought numerous times. Your mother cheated on me numerous times, and I left your mother a few times and got involved with the mafia. We didn't have much in common, but the love we had for each other was still there. It took us a while to reconnect, but when that happened, everything fell apart. Our first child is Jacob, your brother. He was a decent child, and he loved your mother so much. Jacob took most of my traits, and your mother disliked that. When we separated for a short period of time, Jacob stayed with your mother to protect her. I was unaware that your mother brought a guest over, and that's when she started having an affair. She got tired of Jacob one day, so her companion shot Jacob so he could have your mother without having a child nearby. I lost my mind when I returned, and I was unable to do anything. I'm sorry for being such a horrible father to you and your brother! I'm a failure, I'm worthless, and I couldn't protect the ones I love! I didn't inform you because I didn't want to ruin your mind."

"Father, you said you refused to ruin my mind, but if you were watching me all this time, you would realize my mind, heart, soul, and body is now corrupted! I am not the young child you knew me as anymore. I lost a grip on my soul and gave it to the devil for redemption. How can you save me or stop my mind from being corrupt? I never wanted any of this to happen to me, but reality kicked in, and here I am now! So, Father, please spare me the headache and give me useful information so I can end this nightmare. I can't change what occurred in the past. I'm sorry to hear you were deceived by Mother. However, I feel nothing except pain!" I said, baring my heart to him.

My father came closer to me and hugged me. I felt content temporarily. He told me that it would be the last time he'd spend time with me until I broke free of the devil's grasp. My father gave me the last words that he said to Mother: "Our child, Jacob, is now dead because of you. You took away a part of me that I will never get back. Why did you do that, my love? Please tell me why. I thought you wanted to be a family together and become one until death separated us. I guess I was wrong all this time, my love. I found out that you cheated on me numerous times without hesitation. I'm a fool to believe that you actually love me. However, Mary, I love you unconditionally, and I want the best for you. We went through thick and thin and faced adversity together. I know I'm not always there by your side, but just know I love you no matter what. I wish to have another child with you. Our next child will be named David! Yes, that is a perfect name. I want David to be an intelligent, outspoken young individual who can lead and set examples for others. I forbid the devil to interfere with David's journey. I know our child will be successful and happy! No matter what happens between us, let's give David the best childhood ever."

My father began vanishing as he held on to me. The void in my heart also vanished, and I was back in reality. It felt like a hole had been plugged, and I had a reason to fight. All that time, my father loved me unconditionally despite the bond we had. It's amazing how one man can endure so much pain! "I'm sorry, Father, for being so ungrateful! I must become a better man than you and prove to you that I can be a great man."

Everything happens for a reason, no matter how critical the situation may be. However, the situation I was in is critical from many perspectives. If I tried to turn back now and undo my wrongs or repent for my sins, I would never reunite with my soul and truly meet my demise. Every action truly comes with a consequence, no matter what route you take. I'd spent most of my life in regret and being skeptical about every action I take. The energy you put in the world will return to you ten times fold. It doesn't matter where you go or what you do; you can't run away from your faith. I cried so easily; I was emotionally compromised. My life had just begun, but it already felt like I was at the end of my journey. Isolating myself from reality and holding on to the painful memories was demolishing what was left of my soul slowly but surely. Could my body endure any more pain? Would I ever find someone to give me genuine love like my parents gave me, and how would I become humane once more? I could remember vividly the last time I smiled. It was such a memorable event in my life, but it felt like I would never experience it again.

I suddenly snapped back into reality, and a new piece of the puzzle was added. It's amazing how random events can align together to reveal the truth. I began walking out the hallway to exit the old man's house, deciding to return home to rest a bit. As I walked back home, my uncle drove past me with an unusual smirk on his face when he noticed me. Without saying hello to me, my uncle drove off without hesitation! Had I offended or inconvenienced him? I decided not to bother about that at the moment.

I finally got to my house and entered. I immediately noticed a blank envelope with a letter inside it. I became skeptical because I wondered who would take their valuable time to write me a letter. The letter read, "David, I noticed you gathered a great deal of information throughout these few days. I think it is time for you to give up on your quest and enjoy the little time you have to live on earth. I love you, so I don't want things to get physical! Please, David, stop pursuing the truth, or I will alter your journey. From the time you came into this world, I kept an eye on you. I know how determined you are to solve this mystery, and I know what you sacrificed. I wasn't expecting you to go to that extent, David. I commend you for sacrificing your soul, but your journey ends here. Please don't come outside tomorrow, or you'll have a visitor!"

I had been threatened to remain inside and to end my journey. I gave up everything to reveal the truth. I won't allow an insignificant piece of trash stop me! The rage I isolated was resurfacing again, and I craved bloodshed as before. It seemed that no matter what route I took, I would have to end someone's life. As the sun disappeared and the moon appeared, I lay in bed contemplating my next move. Shall I step out gun blazing or remain passive? Either way, someone was going to rest in peace very shortly! Time went by rapidly as I got lost in thought. I began falling asleep, but an unusual sound came from my window. It felt like someone was monitoring me. I might be wrong. Shortly, a letter flew into my room with blood stains on it. "I'm watching you, boy, don't allow your emotions to fool you!" it read. From that moment, I knew I had to fight back. My guns were covered with dust due to being idle for so long. Those suicidal thoughts became a dream, and my subconscious and conscious mindset was fixed on killing my enemies. Every movement was being monitored, so I decided to cover all the windows mid-way and isolate myself. I created dolls that looked identical to me, and I attached bombs inside of the dolls. My dusty guns shined as I cleaned every inch of it and strapped on my bulletproof vest. I would obliterate everyone who stands in my way that day!

As midnight came, I crept next to the window. As I peeked out the window, a red dot appeared on my forehead, so I stepped back. If I made one wrong move, I'd get shot. I quickly ran back to the window and removed the objects blocking the window. I quickly threw the doll at the assassin and detonated it. It was a direct hit, but there was still another assassin. I only had a few seconds to locate the other assassin before he spotted me. Suddenly, I heard a thud from the front door, so I jumped through the window and ran across the lawn. I had no reason to look back now, so I threw a grenade near the gas tank to demolish the house. Seconds later, the house went up in flames, and the last assassin crawled out of the rubble, clinging on to his life. I slowly walked towards him with a M191 pistol pointing directly at him. As I stood over the assassin, he told me, "I was sent to protect you from the truth. All of this isn't personal, kid, but it is for your own good." I became skeptical and paused for a second, but I wouldn't allow my emotions to get the best of me at this moment! The rage inside of me was increasing as I held the cold gun barrel. Sadly, my emotions took control, and I fired the pistol—a direct hit to the head, which splattered his skull. Everything seems to be off, and it doesn't make sense at all!

Every time I took one step forward, an obstacle seemed to place me back ten steps back. Trying to comprehend all of the events was confusing. How can someone know my movements since I was born if the only individuals who knew me well were my parents? Was I missing a piece to the puzzle, or was I that foolish that I could not understand a simple error within my path? All of this was stressful, and I was not making progress! There was one person who I believed could provide answers: my father's friend. It was time to give Jonny a visit.

Jonny lived five blocks away from our house. I wonder if the guy was still alive. As I walked to Jonny's house, I felt a thug, and everything went dark as if I had been plunged into another realm once more. Suddenly, my brother appeared, and we stared at each other while we shed tears. "Brother, you are close to revealing the truth. I'm your guardian angel until you regain your soul. I'm the only thing that's keeping you sane. The devil has your soul, but he doesn't have full control of you. I'm the bridge between you both. However, I'm not sure how long I can endure the devil bombarding. He plans to keep your soul even after you fulfill your duty. It's all a trap, bother! Whatever you do, don't trust our close relatives! Dad was deceived by many due to the trials and tribulations he encountered. Fight back, kill all who stand in your way. This will be the last time we speak. My spiritual energy is decreasing as I protect you. I love you, brother. Take care!" As my brother left, I regained my consciousness. I guessed I was near the end of my journey. No matter what happened, I seemed to lose everyone I cared about. Ashes to ashes, dust to dust, will the pain ever subside, and will I be happy inside? With a void inside of me and blood stains on my hand, I wondered if I was destined to take this path of redemption. Nobody deserves to live the way I was living!

So many questions but so few answers. A young boy on the path of destruction, chained by his tormented soul. He had one chance to redeem himself, one chance to uncover the truth, and one final push to end the nightmare. It was a treacherous road with little support, no one to confide in, and a heart consumed by a void. God only gives his toughest battles to his strongest soldiers, but I doubted being worthy of his blessings after the damage I'd done. I wanted to change my mindset. I craved a better life, and I longed to end this nightmare. But everything happens for a reason, so I had to endure until I could overcome my trials and tribulations. The word "love" is a dangerous word to toy with. By adding a bit of love to the equation, it can be easy to manipulate or motivate someone. Sadly, I didn't truly understand the nature of love.

I was two blocks away from Johnny's house. As I walked, a black crow flew above me as if following me. But I was fixated on the task I'd set for myself, so I didn't pay attention to the crow. I finally arrived at Johnny's house, and it looked deserted. I knocked on the door several times, but no one answered. An old woman, his neighbor, told me that Johnny hadn't left the house for weeks. It was such a strange situation. Why would Johnny stay inside for so long unless he's hiding? When no one was looking, I broke into his house to investigate. I had come too far to go back empty-handed. As I crept through the window, I smelled a familiar scent. The smell of death assaulted my nostrils, and my heart raced. The smell led me to the living room, where Johnny was sitting with his rib cage exposed. His heart was split in half and stuffed in his mouth. An inhumane way to kill someone, but I'm used to it by now. Why would someone kill Johnny unless his past caught up with him? Or someone is trying to keep me away and prevent me from finding the truth? But this won't stop me. I will find the truth. There's no point in staying in Johnny's house since he was dead. But there was a safe with my father's nickname beside Johnny. I assume someone tried to open the safe, but Johnny refused to give them the password. Everything was so suspicious these days, and nothing made sense. I entered a word my father told me to remember since I was seven. The word is "redemption". My father told me it would be the key to ending what he started if his past caught up with him. The safe clicked open. In the safe, there were documents that contained family records, gold, my father's signature M191 pistol, and a letter. The letter stated that a family member betrayed my father and sent the mafia after my parents. My uncle was the suspect. All this time, I'd been within reach of my target, and I didn't realize it. What a fool I was for not analyzing my surroundings better.

The search for the culprit was over, and it was time to focus on a sole purpose. All my efforts weren't futile, and I could finally get closer to ending this nightmare. Another chapter in my life was about to begin, and I wondered if I could endure more pain and suffering. Most young individuals are living a life stress-free, so why do I have to endure such pain and watch the ones I love die repeatedly? Sacrifice is necessary to gain something much greater. I know that well since I sacrificed my soul to the devil. However, every action comes with a consequence, whether you are ready to endure it or not. Furthermore, do not be a pessimist nor dwell on negativity. There are many ways to overcome an obstacle. Choose wisely and be free!

CHAPTER 4

HOT & HEAVY

As time progressed, I began to lose a grip on my life entirely. Each day, I committed a crime. I would shed blood and tears due to the amount of tension my body and mind were enduring. It is amazing how someone can love unconditionally and have negative intentions towards you. Anyone can provide love. However, no one's obligated to be loyal to you! Why should I create new bonds with an individual if it will be severed without hesitation and I'll be left with a broken heart and corrupt subconscious mindset? Life is truly filled with unsolved mysteries; however, it is a beautiful place filled with individuals with selfish mindsets. I want to eradicate every last soul that creates mischief and violence. In the end, I would save myself for last and end it with a gunshot wound and a smile on my face. Sadly, it seemed to be a dream at that moment, and I wanted to end the nightmare I was in! One last jump to the end, the source of all my troubles and the twist that changed my life. It was time to chase down my enemy and devour his feelings!

Words aren't enough to express how excited I was to have a proper route to end this madness. I couldn't stop grinning and twitching due to my excitement. I could visualize the look on my uncle's face when I got a hold of him. I'd rip his skin from his flesh, force him to enlighten me about my father's past, and explain why he killed my parents. I wanted to watch him suffer just how I suffered! The walls would be painted red with his blood, and the sound of his screams would be soothing music to my ears. Before I ended his life, I had to cleanse my path. Numerous bad memories, regretful moments, and a corrupted heart can lead anyone astray.

After analyzing the past events, I finally understood why my uncle was behaving strangely. Looks can truly be deceiving, and the individuals you love so much tend to bring destruction to your life. Uncle Jimmy was the first to come to my aid right after my parents died. He always seemed to be near whenever something occurred. I always knew Uncle Jimmy as the silent type, but I wondered why he was like that. It all makes sense now. I had trials and tribulations all because of my uncle. Dark, lonely nights sitting in the cold room became a repeated cycle. Many nights, I starved and cried due to a lack of support and food. My soul was sacrificed to solve this mystery and avenge my parents! Now, it felt like all of those events weren't necessary, and time was wasted. It was futile to regret my past decisions because it was too late to turn back. I am the man I am because of the trials and tribulations I encountered. No one is truly to blame because I chose to seek revenge rather than walk away. It truly was what it was, and life goes on!

When one is a child, life is much easier. No true responsibilities, adults will support you and fight your battles, the world isn't bombarding you as yet, and you won't be discriminated against for all of your actions. There is so much pain in the world, especially when you are looking at the world through broken glass. Most people would cut you down and watch you bleed out. Turn off all the lights, and you will witness all the demons surrounding everyone. Will you drain out the bad energy with drugs, alcohol, or meditation, or will you commit suicide to end your journey? Whatever it is, do what's best for you and smile!

Uncle Jimmy usually stayed home with my cousins until 7 p.m. when their mother returned home from work. He would take his usual stroll to the bar two blocks from his house to grab a six-pack of beer. This will be the perfect time to ambush him and drag him into the bush. However, this was easier said than done. He knew that I was solving the mystery of my parent's death. He knew I was willing to go beyond my limitations to make ends meet. Uncle Jimmy must have been aware that I might hunt him down. Either way, if he became suspicious and attempted to run, I would make it rain bullets on his position. It is depressing to know that family is one of the main reasons why your rate of success in life cuts down to little or nothing.

As the sunset fell, I quickly ran a block away from the local bar Uncle Jimmy attends. I hid behind a dark alley and waited for my uncle to arrive. Thirty minutes later, I noticed a man walking close to my position. He was walking slowly with his hands in his pocket and whistling. It seemed to be Uncle Jimmy, so I peeked out and confirmed that it was him. However, something seemed off. It was silent, and he was the only person walking on this corner. This seemed like a fishy situation, but I refused to miss this opportunity. Uncle Jimmy finally came close enough for me to snatch him. I gripped him from behind and pressed the gun on his back. With one shot, the bullet would pierce his skin and damage his heart from behind. However, it truly seemed that Uncle Jimmy knew I would track him down. He pulled a cobra derringer 9mm out of his pocket and positioned it near my pelvis. I had fallen into his trap, and it became an eye for an eye situation. Uncle Jimmy began talking and told me to calm down before I made another mistake.

"David, I know what you are thinking, but there is more than one side to the story, and there is a bigger threat waiting for you. I should've said something earlier, but I had to remain silent. Your parents made a horrible decision before you were born, and in the end, your brother met his demise. Your parents sacrificed your older brother to save themselves. However, it didn't end there, and your parents had many altercations. You were born into this world to end their problems, but I did something that changed both yours and my life. I demolished the mafia alpha male and brunt down his warehouse. I told the mafia to keep your parents out of any altercation, so they focused all of their attention on me. However, they were unable to locate me, so they went back to your parents. Your parents decided to sacrifice you to regain peace. To stand on the sidelines and watch another innocent child die due to their selfish actions didn't sit well with me. The night I killed your parents, I decided to save you and start a war with the mafia to end it all. I knew you would hunt me down, and I never sent anyone after you. If you encountered friction from a few individuals, then that was the mafia. David, after I killed your parents and initiated the war with the mafia, I sacrificed my soul to the devil just as you did. I'm sorry, David, you have the right to kill me as I stand. Please do not continue this path, but once I die, the mafia will bombard you."

All of this was traumatizing, and I was unable to pull the trigger. I loosened my grip and let go of Uncle Jimmy. We sat down, and he told me that he had one more mission to redeem himself. Uncle Jimmy dropped his gun and requested mine. I became skeptical, but I gave him my gun. He pointed the gun to his temple and told me, " I'm sorry. Be safe, and please save my soul from the devil." Uncle Jimmy pulled the trigger and splattered his brains on the street. I didn't know if I should be content or depressed. Every time I took two steps ahead, I was pushed back ten steps!

Murder consumed my mind. My heart was engulfed in darkness, and all I knew was pain. Who truly knows what is right and wrong? I knew I was not perfect, but no one could discriminate against me for taking action. A gun with a full clip, bullet shells scattered all over the streets, and I would slide on all my enemies! I asked God for help, but I drifted further in the path of destruction. My enemies will face all of the consequences; they shall know the true meaning of pain before I disintegrate their brains. *God, I know I'm wrong, but I am going to send your children back to you*, I resolved. I did not deserve a second chance nor to be saved by such a pure individual. When I faced my demise, I would accept the consequences and die with my regrets. I didn't wish for this life, but I refused to allow my enemies walk on this earth without suffering! Furthermore, each person I killed would become a memory. It seemed that I'd never abandon this treacherous path, but I must see it through until I end this nightmare.

I was unsure how I would locate the head of the mafia to burn their hideouts down to the ground, but I would allow time to reveal the stepping stones. In due time, someone would find me and try to exterminate me. However, I didn't think I was prepared to go against the mafia. One man against an organized criminal organization is suicide. However, I was willing to go beyond the limitations I set upon myself to make my enemies suffer. I gave my soul to the devil as a down payment to our agreement.

My house was destroyed, and I was truly alone now. It is time to relocate, so Johnny's house will be my new home for now. I walked inside the house and realized Johnny's body had disappeared. I didn't know if someone was trying to hide evidence or if something unexplainable had happened while I was gone. Either way, it was not important at the moment. I placed bear traps around the house and soaked sharp steel rods in poison to ambush an intruder. Some of the steel rods are placed in areas where intruders would usually try to enter. If my traps were successful, an intruder would suffer from poisoning and would be unable to remove the bear trap from their foot.

It had been a while since I took a nap, so I deserved one before I encountered another obstacle. I took a shower and then jumped in bed. The warmth of the bed caused me to reminisce about my old bed. As I inhaled and exhaled, my eyes became heavy, and I slowly drifted asleep.

My eyes fluttered open, and I woke up with the devil beside me. No words are exchanged, and the tension is high. Things were heating up, and it was almost time to end this nightmare. When I returned to the land of the living, the true battle would commence.

CHAPTER 5

WAR

L ife is filled with mysterious individuals and events. One second, you can be living your best life with your loved ones, then suddenly, you can be on your death bed within seconds. Tomorrow is not promised to anybody, and every time we open our eyes, we are given a chance to do wonderful things in life. A person's life tends to be valued by what they can bring to the table. Most individuals aren't able to provide and are placed in the poor classification group. Life is beautiful. However, this world is filled with people with insidious intentions. When will society release all the negativity and fill the world with positivity? Sometimes, it's better to isolate yourself from society rather than to try to help individuals who will discriminate against you and gun you down for your opinion. Either way, it's your life, and you can decide which path to take!

The encounter with the devil left me with a vivid memory and reminded me that things are coming to an end. I was finally back into reality, and nothing had happened while I was asleep. It seemed too quiet, which is odd. I was bothered that Uncle Jimmy took his life in front of me. I had thought I could finally end this nightmare by killing Uncle Jimmy, but I was wrong. My existence is futile from my perspective, and I'm useless! I was forced to mature. I had no choice but to embrace life's bombarding and stand on my own two feet. Uncle Jimmy took my parents away from me, but he also protected me. How could I hold a grudge against him for trying to love me in his own way? He made me the man of the house and left me behind in this cold world so suddenly. I anticipated locating the head of the mafia. And when I did, I would watch the fire burn off their flesh and reminisce about my family.

What seems a bit off is that I noticed a tattoo on Uncle Jimmy's arm, which seems similar to the tattoos on the assassin's arms. It looked similar to the tattoos on the assassins' arms: a lion with an X on the forehead in a circle. I didn't pay much attention to the tattoo or think it was an important clue. But I remembered seeing that tattoo on the wall of a building when I was younger. It was near my house, but I couldn't recall exactly where. Still, I could use this hint as a lead and hope it would point me in the right direction. It was surprising how most of the events that happened were in my neighborhood, and I never noticed them until the day I lost my parents. Life is truly easier when you're a child with no worries.

All I could do was walk around my neighborhood and prepare for war—one boy equipped with two assault rifles with hollow tips loaded, one M191 pistol, a short cutlass, and a bullet proof vest. My enemies would scream for their loved ones while I empty the magazine. Every individual with the lion tattoo branded on their skin would receive the penalty: a slow, painful death! The morgue business will have a drastic boom. I knew I was not the only child suffering from this organization's corruption. To end it all, I would erase any remaining memory of the mafia. It was a heavy responsibility to place on myself. However, it must be done to end my nightmare and to prevent another child from going through what I went through.

My parents left me with such a burden on my shoulders. I guess it was truly meant this way. I thought they unconditionally loved me without an ounce of sinister intentions. My parents kept me around to make things easier for themselves, which is selfish. The unconditional love I have for my parents will not deteriorate. However, I would never forgive them for what they did to me and my brother. However, everything happens for a reason, and our parents sacrificed us to protect themselves—such a tragic way to be manipulated by your own parents.

Still, life must go on, and I couldn't turn back the clock to undo what has been done. This is not the way a young boy should live, nor something he/she should experience at a young age. Life has a mysterious way of reconditioning an individual mindset. Nobody wants to die. Nobody wants to take responsibility for their actions, and nobody wants to see their love one die in front of them. The heart is such a soft organ, and it can be destroyed in seconds. I wondered how things would be once I ended this nightmare. I doubt the devil will let me off so easily without a fight. My life would never be the same again, and I was willing to accept it. However, I knew my brother would not allow me to give up on myself so easily.

Three days had passed, and nobody tried to break into the house or kill me. Maybe they are watching outside, waiting for me to reveal myself. The silence was unsettling, and the air was heavy. The feeling was similar to when the assassins came to my house to kill me. However, I haven't received any warnings or seen someone stalk the house. Perhaps I was being too paranoid, or I was not worth the trouble. Whatever the case, my intuition was feeding my subconscious mindset with negative visualizations. I was going through a constant cycle of negativity and misery. Sometimes, I regretted making a deal with the devil. I signed my own demise in the worst way possible. I should've listened to my brother, Uncle Jimmy, and Johnny. I dug so deep in the path of destruction and heartbreak that I was unable to turn back. I desired the truth; however, the truth made things worse. I know the truth should set you free, but it was not the same for my situation.

As I gathered more information, I realized my life had become worse. I truly wasn't supposed to unveil the truth or execute my plans. I made a horrible mistake. I could've left things how they were and minded my own business. Nevertheless, it was too late for regret! Regret wouldn't change the outcome nor help me accomplish my goal. Only the Lord and the Devil knew how the extent of my pain. It was difficult to continue this path with so much weight on my shoulders. It felt like an elephant was leaning on my shoulders while I was trying to walk along my path. I guess I was emotionally compromised due to all of the events in my life. I was unable to remain stable in all ways, and I could feel the void consuming everything around me. I sensed that my life was coming to an end very shortly! I may have been wrong; however, to me, I was already dead from the moment I gave the Devil my soul. For most of my life, I have witnessed people dish out negative energy without hesitation. Yet, at that moment, I was doing the exact thing I watched others do. I deserved a slow, painful death that would cause me to reminisce about the few good moments I had in the past before I took my final breath. To come into this cruel world to be used as a tool is a disgrace. My embers shall burn through my enemies' skin and leave a deep scar on society before my embers meet their demise.

Nothing had occurred so far, and I found it strange. I had become used to death and destruction following me wherever I went, no matter the circumstance. Why was the neighborhood so quiet, and why wasn't anyone after me anymore? I peeped into the window to analyze the area and realized everybody was missing, which was also strange. The road would usually be filled with children, garbage, and grown folks on their porches talking to their associates. However, as I looked around, I saw that there was not a person in plain sight. Someone did something sinister in order to change the environment so quickly. If I was the only individual in the area, my enemies could kill me without any witness or distraction. I had to investigate this awkward situation. It was time to go back outside and explore. It may not be a wise choice, but I didn't believe I had any other choice! I had come this far towards achieving the goal; I could not stop now. Either way, it was not like I could walk away from this life so easily anymore. Such was my life; I dug my own grave in this beautiful world.

As the sun rosed and lit up the neighborhood, I got prepared to finally leave the house. My guns were fully loaded, I sharpened my knife to the best of my ability, and I wore a bulletproof vest underneath my shirt. As I walked down the road, I began to feel a stench aura coming from an alley where drugs were sold. Usually, the grown folks would warn us from getting near that area, but I was alone, so nobody could try to alter my course. I walked near the alley and discovered a stack of bodies in a pool of blood. Flies and maggots swarmed in and around the bodies. The smell alone was hard to withstand, and I was not sure who would kill three generations of people within three days. I knew I was a cold-hearted young individual. However, I did not have the courage to attempt genocide so easily. I might be on a path of destruction and plan to wipe out the mafia, but I don't involve innocent individuals in my mess. To give these people a proper send-off, I poured fuel all over their bodies and set them on fire. As I sat near the burning bodies, it felt like someone was watching me from afar. It was as if I was doing exactly what they wanted me to do. I may have been paranoid, but I could sense that something was going to happen very shortly! However, to witness this inhumane sight and to be the one to burn their bodies placed me in a nonchalant state. I couldn't care less now if someone was watching me. If that person wanted me dead, I would've been dead already. It was time to play along to my enemies' game and place a trap beside their trap to discombobulate their mental state.

It took five hours to burn every last person down to ashes completely. I collected their ashes and placed them in a five-gallon water bottle. This should be sufficient to scatter their ashes in a nice place. The hill near the edge of town was the perfect place to release their ashes, but that was where my father carried me one day to meet an associate of his. I still found it amazing that I hadn't encountered an individual with a serious intention to kill me. It was like I was being spared from death by the mafia, but they remained close, analyzing my actions. There have been a few mild attempts to hurt me because I've been vulnerable enough to be killed several times. As I walked further along this path, the questions increased, but the answers to the questions decreased. It all felt like a facade, and when I took four steps forward, something would place me ten steps back. Someone was trying to keep me at bay while remaining on the sidelines. I thought killing my uncle would solve the problem, but life gave me a different perspective, and the journey became more treacherous. There were more secrets I hadn't yet uncovered, so I had no choice but to continue moving forward. The walk to the hill took me roughly fifteen minutes. I had been walking all over town like a headless chicken. I wondered if people thought I was crazy because I was frequently all over the town. It was all becoming tiresome. When would this journey end? When would someone take me out of my misery? Why did my enemy decide to remain in the shadows while I wandered around town looking for clues? I felt like I was in a rat maze. I wanted to give up.

A child on the path of destruction with a fading ember in his heart. An ocean emerged in his eyes, and the void increased within. Why force the light to shine upon you if darkness kept you safe? Why remain in darkness if the light will protect you from negativity? Nevertheless, the ember will slowly die, and everything will become a facade. Sunny days and dark nights, everything must end.

I was three minutes away from the hill, and I noticed crows flying above the hill in a circular formation like something was dead. It felt strange for something like that to happen as I was making my way up the hill. It was a little ironic that something always seemed to be waiting for me the moment I appeared in a particular direction. Maybe it was destined to happen, or perhaps I was about to fall into someone's trap. My soul was in the devil's possession, so my life truly didn't matter as much anymore because I sold myself to save the people I loved. Was I a fool for such selfish actions? Maybe I was, but it was too late to contemplate it.

I finally arrived at the hill, and a gentleman dressed in a black suit with a ghost face mask stood in my direction as if he was awaiting my arrival. The gentleman dashed toward me without hesitation, and within seconds, I was face down to the floor. The ashes I collected dropped as well, but the container was still in one piece. My head got pressed between the floor and the man's boot. He twisted my arms backward to the point where I thought he would dislocate them. As much as I desired to retaliate, I was unable to move or fight back because it would make the situation worse. I had finally encountered someone who was determined to put a stop to my journey. The pain increased, but the guy held me in place without uttering a single word. My head felt like it was on a press machine slowly being crushed. Maybe, if I submitted, I would finally die, and this long, treacherous journey would end.

The thought of dying triggered my emotional state and made me emotionally compromised. I lost sight of the goal I placed upon myself and the mission the devil assigned me. Had I become soft or discouraged? Why was I searching for an easy way out rather than completing the mission? I was pathetic; I allowed a stranger to pin me to the ground. I began to cry, becoming even more vulnerable. The man finally decided to speak, and what he said sent chills down my spine, "I can grant you your death wish now, but I prefer to see you suffer a little more. I've been watching to solve your puzzle, but everything you know now is just the tip of the iceberg. You thought you were hunting me down, but I've been watching you from the shadows since the day you started this doomed quest. You are nothing but a pawn in your parents' twisted game. This is your last chance to turn back before you face the truth that will shatter your world. I am the one you seek. I am the mafia boss. And killing me won't end your story. It will only begin your nightmare."

After he said his last word, I felt a large object bashed against my head. I blacked out, and he walked away. I had thought I was progressing, but I had fallen deeper into a trap laid for me since birth. My subconscious and unconscious mindsets were discombobulated again. I was unconscious, yet I moved freely in my consciousness.

Every step was like taking a leap over a snake pit filled with guns pointed at me. The devil was on my shoulder, whispering sinister thoughts to me. The mafia boss was currently watching each step I took, and it seemed I had lost a grip on myself. Maybe meditating will help me regain a bit of sanity or peace of mind. However, I must travel deep into my unconscious mindset to limbo to meditate without the devil interfering. I was still unconscious, so it wouldn't be difficult to enter my sanctuary. It felt like five minutes had passed since I drifted into my subconsciousness. I was able to re-enter the void I first appeared in when my brother tried to reconnect with me spiritually. This time, neither my brother nor my father was around. The void became bigger since I was alone, but it was better than being conscious and being chased by my demons. I began my meditation by sitting down and taking deep breaths, slowly breathing in and out. Gradually, I began to hear my heartbeat and reminisce about my family. Despite my family being filled with negativity, I still love them regardless of what they did. I may be a fool to love someone who brought great misery upon my life, but they were all I had. It's depressing to know that all your loved ones are dead, and you have nobody to vent to. I had no one to help guide me back on the right path or comfort me at my lowest. I was a young boy in a cold-hearted world who was lost, confused, and cornered by the enemy. Despite being in my sanctuary, I was still bombarded by the thoughts of my nightmares and reality. Still, I continued to sit and breathe slowly.

A warmth spread on my back. I spun around but saw nothing. When I faced forward again, my mother stood before me like a dream. We locked eyes as if meeting for the first time. She embraced me and whispered an apology. I was baffled. Why was she sorry?

She looked at me and said, "David, I've been watching you suffer since your father and I died. You've learned so much, but you have many questions. I'll tell you everything, but hurry. I'm fading fast. Your father and I made terrible mistakes. We sold your and your brother's souls to save ours. We lived recklessly and fell in with the wrong crowd. We became monsters and neglected you. The man you're chasing is the devil himself. You can't escape him unless you enter his realm and kill him. The Yin side of you and your brother's soul are his prisoners. It's too late for us, but you can still save yourself. We're better off dead; at least we're free from his grip. Goodbye, my son. You've grown so strong and independent. We love you, even if you don't love us anymore." My mother quickly vanished, and there was silence once more.

I was on a treacherous path now. It all made sense why I was always two steps behind my enemy. Everyone who crossed my path died. The devil was on my shoulder, pulling the strings. He set me up from birth like it was my fate to fight this bloody battle. He must have known I was coming for him. I was pathetic for falling for his game. I was a menace for what I had done. How could I seek God's forgiveness? But I had to end this nightmare. Whatever comes next, I was prepared to take it.

I had been running blindly, following his cues. I now knew why I hit a wall every time I tried to move forward. I clung to memories that held me back. Who could blame me for choosing my haven over this hell? But those memories are the link to my loved ones. I was torn between heaven and hell, between my subconscious and unconscious. Some days, I fought with my demons. Some days, I fled from them and dwelled on my past. My story is a mess. I was a lost soul in the world of the living and limbo.

My path was almost over, and I did not know what lay ahead, but I knew I would end this journey. Since I was a tool for the devil and had been manipulated all this time, it was time to play a game. If you can't beat your opponent, join them. I went back to what was left of my home and sat down on the rubble. Being idle will infuriate the devil, and I would have to meet him in person. Although he was monitoring my actions, he had no choice but to confront me. I had had enough of the bloodshed, the lies, the deception, and heartbreaks. Materialistic things, the thought of responsibility, selfishness, and fear destroyed my family, or maybe it revealed their true nature. Nevertheless, it was my responsibility to end this journey my parents started.

I was in a dark place, alone. Or so I thought. A flurry of slashes hit me out of nowhere. Blood gushed from my wounds. My left arm shook. The devil appeared before me, and I froze. He was too powerful. My weapons were useless. I was bleeding out. I had one choice but to face death. I charged at him and swung with all my strength. He barely flinched. His eyes were gateways to another world. A sharp staff pierced my stomach and pinned me to the wall like a trophy.

Nothing I did mattered. Why fight a losing battle? Why waste my life on bitterness? Why ruin myself for someone else's happiness? Is this the world we live in? How can it change? What is love, really? We humans are the cause of it all—a dog-eat-dog society in a beautiful world.

I hung from the wall, watching blood drip from my legs. My vision blurred. My energy faded. The devil smiled at me, enjoying my agony. My parents were dead. My brother's soul was trapped with mine. I was left to suffer. How much can one person take? I had one option left: to pray and find peace. Our father who art in heaven, I am a sinner. I have sinned so much. I stained my hands with blood. I ran from the light and followed my parents' footsteps. My soul was in the devil's hands, but I became a menace to society. How can I redeem myself, father? I am not worthy, but you let me choose my path. I am responsible for everything that happened to me after my parents' death. Thank you for everything and more.

My eyes remained closed, and I entered my sanctuary once more. The yang side of me was waiting for my arrival. What a shocking surprise. The yin side for me sat gazing at me with a large flame behind it. Words alone would not help this situation, so I thought it best to show love. Love, something that made me excited to receive. I must protect what was left of me, even if it meant accepting my past. My past would no longer dictate my future, and I would no longer fight a losing battle. My fight was over. I realized I was losing myself. I accepted the broken path I walked on and my past. The yin side of me leaped at me. Then, the yang side of me appeared. "Your brother hid me from all spiritual connections until you were ready. I was hidden in plain sight, but the devil couldn't see me. You are whole. You have the power to end this journey. Free us from this torture. Open your eyes and be free. Pull out the staff and stab the devil in his head. You fought well. Thank you." The world is full of deception and hatred. Love is confused with lust and corruption. Money is the key to people's hearts and minds. When will the world stop and cleanse? Time will tell if we will continue to falter and fall in hell.

As the devil stood before me, I opened my eyes and noticed a smirk on his face. He seemed ready to continue the battle. Did I truly have the power to defeat him, or was this just a facade? I began to remove the staff as the devil stood before me. I pulled out the staff as he watched me. He said nothing, did nothing. He didn't see me as a threat, or was this another trap? He whispered, "You have the will to overcome your challenges, but you let darkness consume your heart, and your hands are stained with blood. You want peace, but you traded your soul for revenge. You will be a tool forever." His words crushed my spirit, and my chest sank.

The tears began to fall one after another without hesitation. The truth can indeed hurt, but it can also set you free. I came too far to falter and to allow words alone to keep me down! I finally pulled the staff out and pierced through the devil's head with swiftness. My heart was beating like a drum, and my palms were sweaty. I finally tasted victory; however, something seemed off. The devil's body wasn't moving, but I still sensed a diabolical aura. Suddenly, I fell to my knees, and as I looked up, I could see those I had killed.

"Young boy, your hands are stained with our blood, your eyes run dry from the tears, and your heart is tangled in a dark place. You overcame a difficult trail and sacrificed so much. Well done. Take each obstacle as a learning experience. Be free and turn your life around for the better. Thank you for assisting us to meet our demise. We've done so many wicked things in life. Run from this life while you have the chance, and smile!"

The devil was dead, and I could finally take a deep breath in. However, I was not worthy to remain in the land of the living. I allowed myself to be manipulated. I took the life of many and walked away from the light. I regretted nothing now; I was just a pawn in this world, and I did my part. I had to complete one more task, and this journey would be over. Without hesitation, I pierced my heart with the spear, placed the pistol to my head, and pulled the trigger with a smile on my face. Death was the only answer. I could finally be with my family in the spiritual realm and make up for those lonely days. My life may have been hectic, but I'm grateful that my brother remained by my side throughout my trials and tribulations. This is the end of my life, dust to dust, ashes to ashes.

About the Author

Cory Alexander Kapril Rolle is a young individual who loves to explore and learn new things. Throughout his youth, he has risen to new heights and faced adversity from all corners—a young mariner exploring the world with an open mindset willing to embark on new horizons.

Made in United States
Orlando, FL
10 December 2024

55384236R00046